RAFE MARTIN

The Language of
BIRDS

ILLUSTRATIONS BY SUSAN GABER

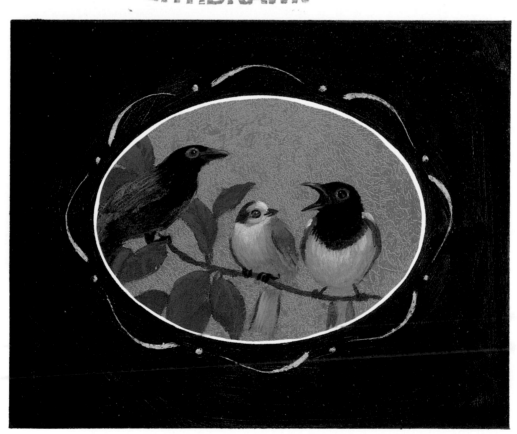

G. P. PUTNAM'S SONS • NEW YORK

Long ago, in a land beyond nine oceans, there lived a wealthy merchant who had two sons. Vasilii was the older, and Ivan, the younger.

One day the merchant said, "The time has come to see how you will fare in the wide world. Here are ten gold coins each. Return in a week and tell me what profit you've gained."

Vasilii took his coins, went to the fair, and spent his money on every pleasure, eating and drinking until his gold was gone.

Ivan went into the green forest where he heard a baby bird cheeping piteously. He found the little bird where it had fallen and returned it to the nest. The mother bird flew around him chirping, "Thank you, kind youth!"

"You're welcome, little mother," said Ivan. "But how is it I understand you?"

"Kindness makes it possible, if just for a moment," answered the bird. "Ask me now for something that a bird might give, for I want to repay you."

Ivan thought. Then he said, "I wish I could *always* understand the language of the birds."

"Done!" chirped the bird in delight. "Come back each day for one week and I'll teach you."

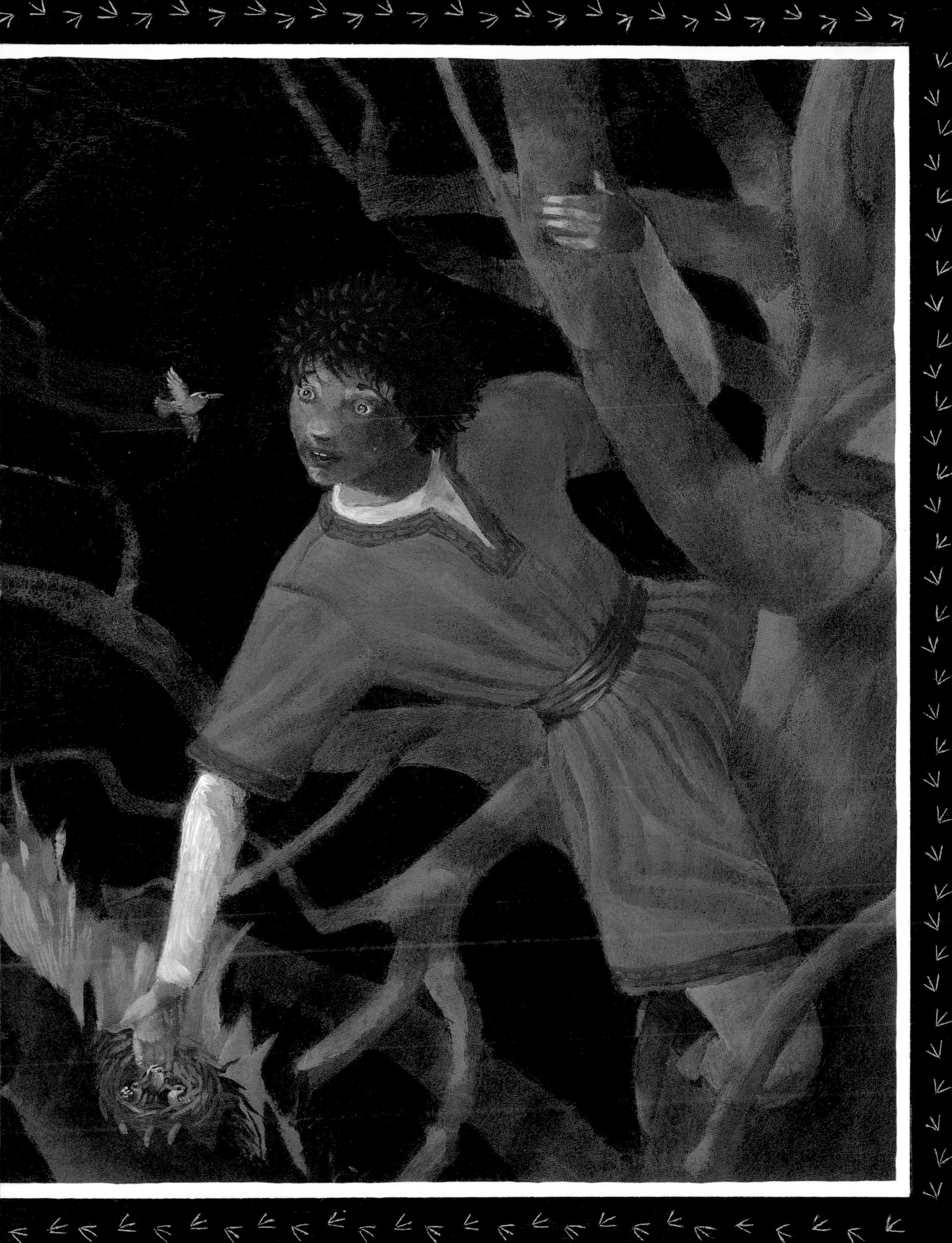

When a week had passed, both sons returned home.

"Boys," said the merchant, "tell me what you have gained, for gain is the most important thing."

"I went to the fair," said Vasilii. "There I spent my gold entertaining the sons of very wealthy merchants. I made no money, but in the future I shall profit from their friendship."

"Excellent!" cried the merchant. "Now, you, Ivan."

"Here are all ten coins back, Father," said Ivan.

"What?" exclaimed the merchant. "But what did you do?"

"I went to the forest," said Ivan, "and learned the language of the birds. It cost nothing."

"No one can understand the language of birds!" shouted the merchant. "Tell me—you who claim to know so much—what is the little wren singing just outside our window?"

"She sings," said Ivan, "that one day I shall be a prince with one hundred horses, each wearing a coat of silver and gold. You shall bring me water in a silver bowl to wash my hands and a fine white cloth to dry them. Vasilii shall tend to my horses."

"Wretch!" roared the merchant in rage. "To invent such a tale! Serve you, indeed! You can spend this night with your friends, the birds. Let them serve you!"

Then Vasilii was brought into the house and feasted royally while Ivan was locked out in the cold and the dark. But little birds brought him berries to eat and sang so sweetly to him that he slept without a care.

The next morning, the merchant said to his sons, "I am sending you to a sea captain I know. Give him this letter and he will give you work. You, Vasilii, will receive a good position. And Ivan, well, he'll find something for you to do."

The two brothers walked along the road. "Why didn't you make up a believable story like mine," asked Vasilii, "instead of telling that outrageous tale of birds?"

"What?" exclaimed Ivan in surprise. "Didn't you spend your money on the merchants' sons?"

"Not at all," said Vasilii. "I spent it all on myself."

"But my story is true!" protested Ivan.

Vasilii just laughed.

When they came to the harbor, the captain read the letter and asked Vasilii, "What would you like to do?"

Vasilii responded, "Besides the captain, who's the most important person aboard?"

"The pilot," answered the captain. "Through knowledge of winds, tides, and currents, the pilot guides us safely to our harbor."

"I know all about such things!" said Vasilii.

"Wonderful!" exclaimed the captain. "The job is yours. Now, Ivan, what do you think your skills are?"

"I'm not sure," said Ivan. "But whatever needs doing, I'll do my best."

"That shows good spirit, at least," said the captain. "For now, take a mop and swab the decks."

Soon the anchor was hoisted, the wind filled the white sails, and the ship set out into the blue sea. A band of cranes flew overhead. Ivan listened to their cries. Then he said to Vasilii, "The cranes warn of a bad storm. They say no ship should leave the harbor."

Vasilii said, "Don't be a fool!"

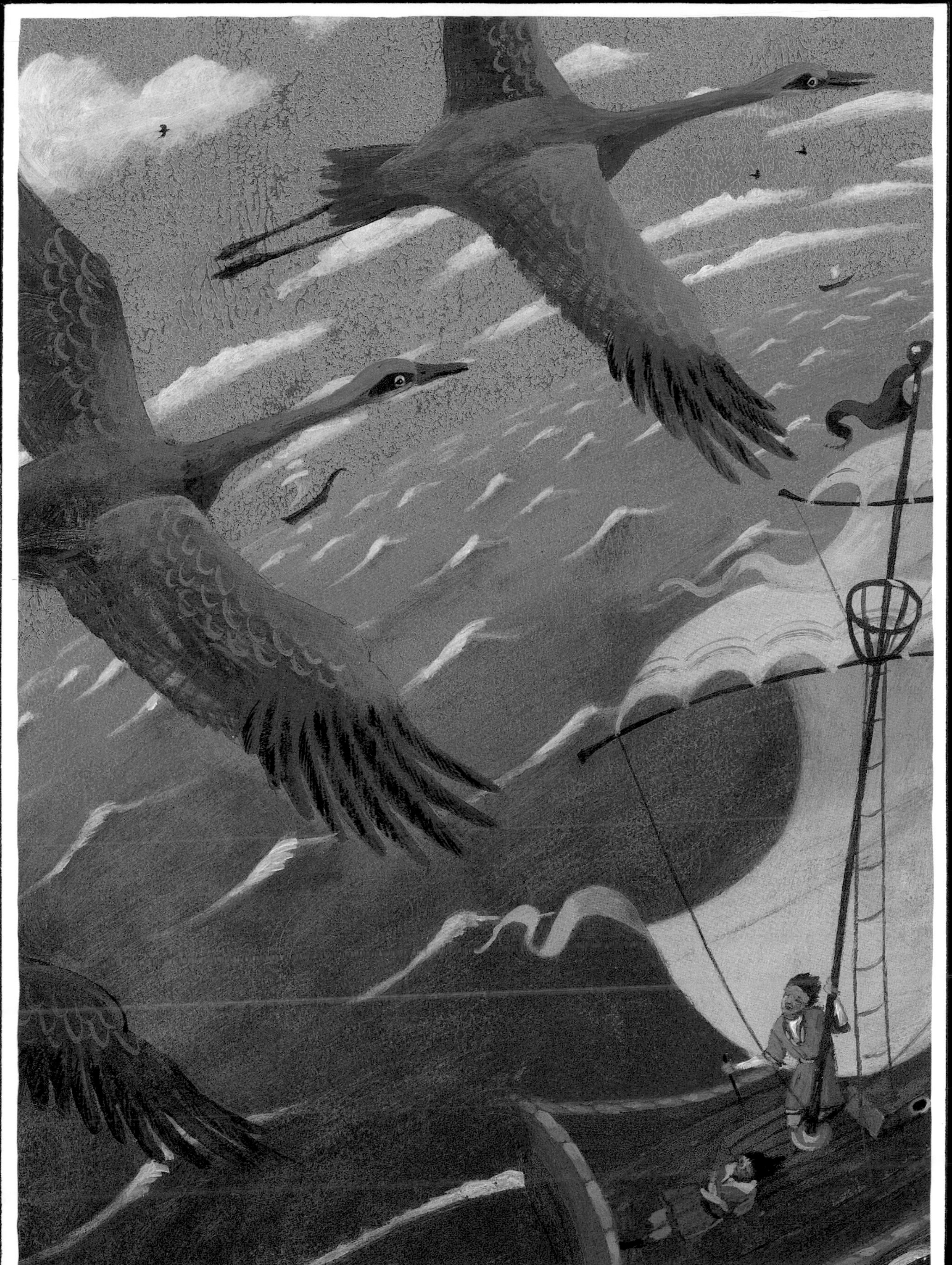

But soon the sky grew dark. The waves rose hungrily and the wind began to howl. The sails were torn to shreds before the storm passed on. The ship limped back to the harbor. The captain stormed at Vasilii, "You are supposed to warn us of such things!"

"It was a freak storm," said Vasilii. "Rig the sails again. It will be safe in the morning."

The next morning, with new sails rigged, the ship set forth once more. A flock of swans flew overhead. Ivan listened. Then he said, "The swans warn that pirates lurk in the cove ahead and that we should turn back before they attack."

"Ridiculous!" snorted Vasilii. But sailors overheard Ivan's warning and went to the captain.

"What's this about pirates?" said the captain, stepping out onto the deck. "And I hear that yesterday we were warned about the storm?"

"My brother is a simpleton and a dreamer," laughed Vasilii. "He thinks he can understand the language of the birds and that they warn him of danger!"

"He was right about the storm," said the captain. "Let's see about the pirates. Lower the ship's boat!" he ordered. The sailors rowed the small boat away.

Soon they could be seen rowing speedily back. "Haul us up," gasped the exhausted sailors. "There are pirates ahead. Ivan has saved us."

"Good youth," said the captain bowing before Ivan. "Please be our pilot. You have saved our lives."

To Vasilii he said, "Take the mop from Ivan. You shall swab the decks."

The next day they set out again. This time, under Ivan's wise guidance, they sailed past all dangers and arrived safely in the kingdom of Czar Demyan—a monarch so wealthy even his horses wore coats of silver and gold.

The captain said, "Stay with us, Ivan. You are the best pilot on the seven seas and your fortune will be made."

Ivan answered, "Thank you. But as I have always loved the green forests, I shall now return to the land."

So the brothers collected their pay, bade farewell to their shipmates, and set off.

In town, they came upon this proclamation:

NIGHT AND DAY THREE CROWS CAW AT THE WINDOW OF
THE GREAT CZAR DEMYAN, KEEPING HIM FROM SLEEP.
THE HERO WHO DRIVES THEM AWAY SHALL RECEIVE THE HAND
OF HIS DAUGHTER IN MARRIAGE AND HALF THE KINGDOM.
THOSE WHO FAIL SHALL DIE.

"Chase three crows and win a princess and half a kingdom!" exclaimed Vasilii. "That's the job for me."

"Careful, brother," said Ivan. "Don't be hasty. Failure means death." But Vasilii was already on his way.

Soon he stood before the czar. "Caw! Caw! Caw!" croaked the crows.

"Silence!" thundered the czar.

"Caw! Caw! Caw!" continued the crows.

"My daughter's hand is yours," sighed the czar, "if you quiet them!"

"Prepare the wedding, Your Majesty," said Vasilii with a bow.

Vasilii went back to town and caught cats: hungry, scrawny, skinny cats. He brought them to the palace and set them free. The cats heard, "Caw! Caw! Caw!" and at once leapt onto walls, clambered up trees, and clawed along vines chasing the three crows, giving them no rest. At last the exhausted crows flapped their weary wings and flew away.

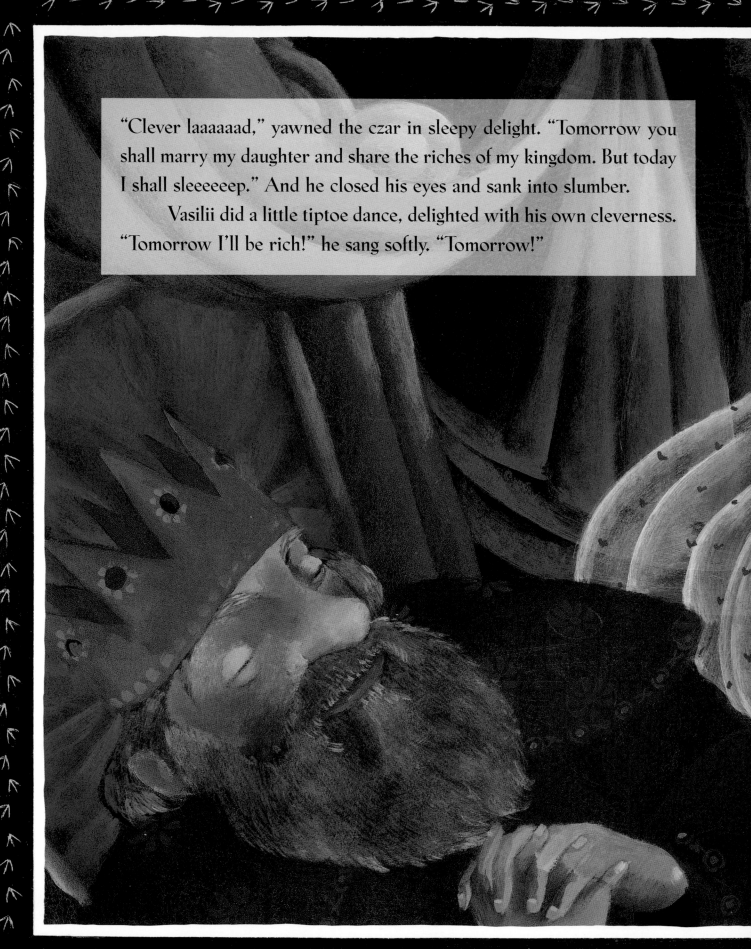

"Clever laaaaaad," yawned the czar in sleepy delight. "Tomorrow you shall marry my daughter and share the riches of my kingdom. But today I shall sleeeeeep." And he closed his eyes and sank into slumber.

Vasilii did a little tiptoe dance, delighted with his own cleverness. "Tomorrow I'll be rich!" he sang softly. "Tomorrow!"

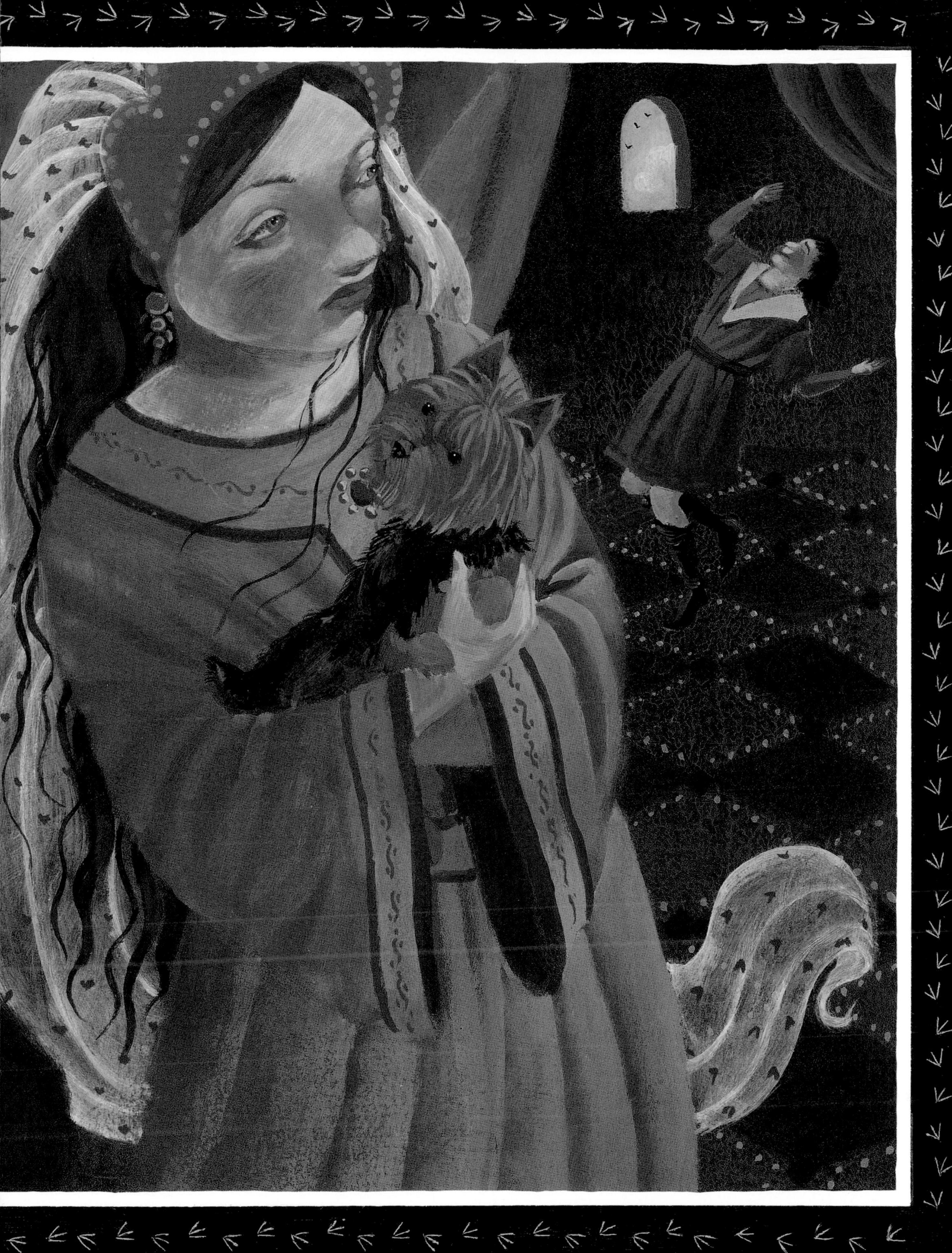

But then, "Caw! Caw! CAW!"

Vasilii stopped singing and dancing. The sky grew dark. "CAW! CAW! CAW!" A huge flock of crows mobbed overhead. They dove at the cats and drove them away. Then the flock flew off, leaving only the three crows again at the czar's window. "Caw!"

The czar woke in anger. "Off with his head!" he roared.

In town, Ivan heard a little bird chirping, "Foolish cats! Beaten by crows!"

"My brother's plan has failed," said Ivan. "I must help him!"

Soon Ivan stood before the czar. "Your Majesty," he said, "I will bring peace."

"Caw! Caw! Caw!" cried the crows. Ivan listened carefully and said, "Sire, the largest crow is the king. Beside him is the queen. Next to her stands their son, the prince. They have come to ask a question which perplexes them: whose advice should a child follow—the father's or the mother's?"

The czar scratched his head and tugged his beard. The three crows watched in silence. At last Czar Demyan sat up on his throne and announced, "Many young warriors arrive at our court hungry and tired, wearing dirty, rumpled, and torn clothes. It's as if they never learned a thing that a mother might teach. They may know how to swing a sword and hurl a spear, but nothing of how to care for themselves! And why shouldn't a daughter learn from her father how to ride a horse, parry a blow, shoot an arrow, and chop firewood? My answer is this: let sons and daughters learn all they can—from both parents."

The crows bowed deeply. Then they flapped their shiny black wings, and flew away

It was quiet! So quiet! The czar clapped his hands, laughed aloud, and said, "The world is filled with wonders. Who would have thought that in my own kingdom was a man who understands the language of the birds? Tomorrow we shall have our wedding, but today is for slee . . ."

"Great Czar," sighed Ivan. "Sadly—for I would like nothing better than to marry the princess—I must ask for a different reward. Please free my brother, Vasilii."

"Father," said the princess, stepping forward. "Do free Vasilii. He must attend the wedding. For tomorrow I shall marry Ivan. My mind is made up. Where shall I ever find another husband who is so kind and who also understands the language of the birds?"

"You are right," agreed the czar. "Guards, free that Vasilii fellow! And now," he yawned, "to sleep!" Ivan and the princess embraced. Vasilii, released from prison, did another little dance for the joy of being free.

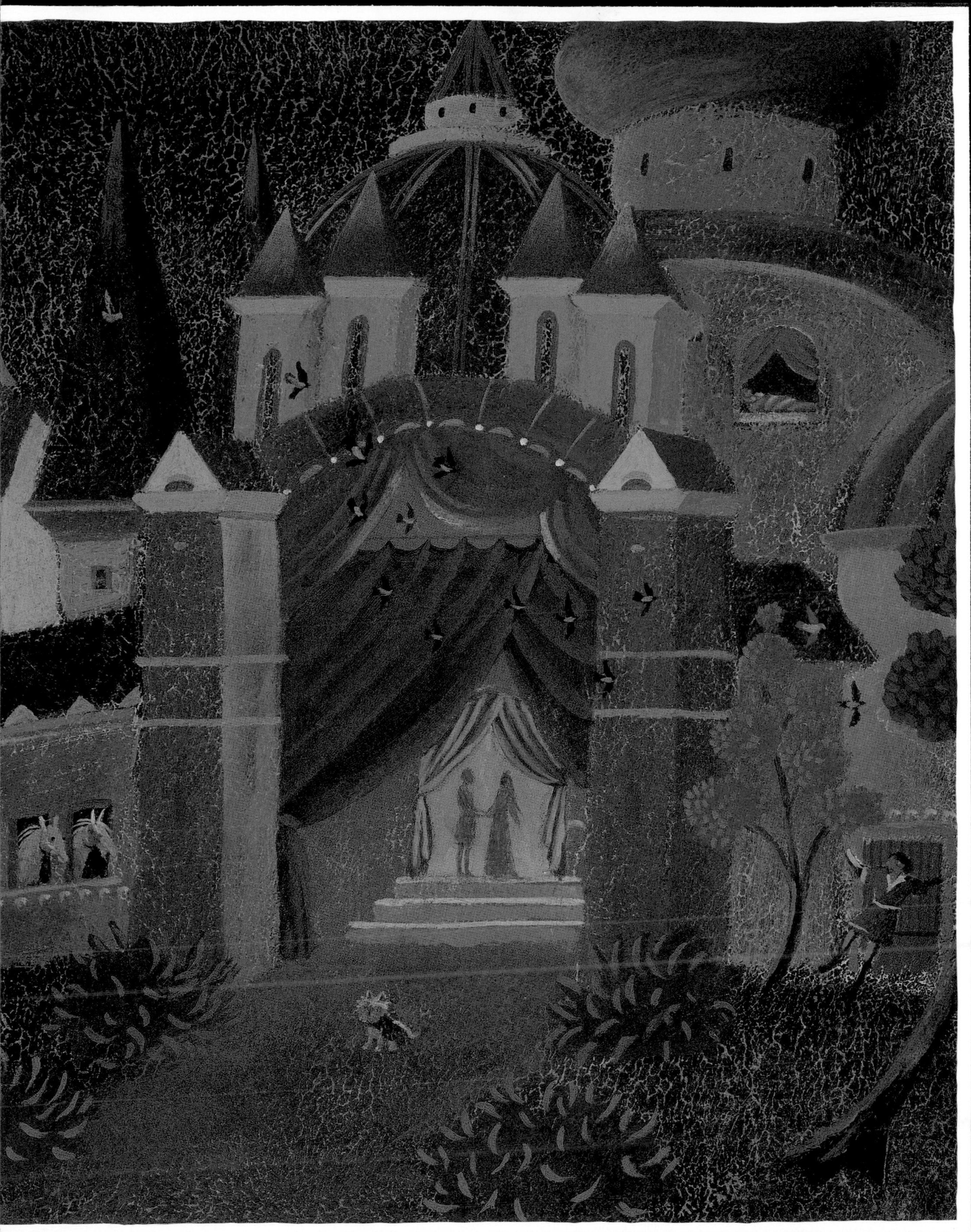

The next day, Ivan and the princess were wed. Now Ivan was a prince with a stable of one hundred horses, each wearing a coat of silver and gold.

One day, as Prince Ivan was setting out, he came across an old beggar. Ivan's heart was moved with pity. "Take care of this old fellow," he said to his attendants. "Give him some new clothes and an easy job."

When Prince Ivan returned, the old man was waiting in fine new clothes. As Ivan got off his horse and approached, the old man burst into tears.

"What is it?" asked Ivan in concern.

"Long ago, before I lost my fortune," said the old man, "I was a rich merchant. I had two sons. The younger told me that one day I would hold a silver bowl and a white cloth for him just as I am doing now for you."

"Father!" cried Ivan in joy. "It is me! I am Ivan, your own son!"

Then how father and son hugged each other and wept tears of joy. The old father came into the palace and lived there with Ivan, his lovely wife, and Vasilii, who now tended the horses.

Indeed, everything turned out just as that little bird had said it would.
And how, you may ask, do I know all this? It's simple. Just the other day a tiny bird flew to my window and told me all about it!

For my Russian grandmothers, Anna Ferber and Minnie Wolf,
and for the tales they told—R. M.

To my Russian grandmother, Lily,
and to my Austrian grandmother, Minnie—S. G.

AUTHOR'S NOTE

I first came across this *skazki*, or folktale, in Post Wheeler's *Russian Wonder Tales* (1912), but brothers like Ivan and Vasilii appear in the myths and tales of cultures worldwide. They demonstrate the range of possibilities and paths within each of us. One is clever, the other, wise. One is selfish, the other, generous. One is a realist, the other, a dreamer. Often the old myths and tales remind us, too, that the dreamer can hold the keys to life. We can hear echoes in our tale of the biblical Joseph. His more worldly brothers mocked his dreams, yet his skill with dreams saves them all in the end.

There are far older notes here as well. Saying someone "understands the language of the birds" is a very ancient way of saying that someone is wise; like a bird, that person's spirit can soar, is beautiful, and is filled with song. It is a way of saying that the heart and mind and spirit are open and awake and that one has found kinship with all life. Bird-costumed Siberian shamans and bird-masked dancers painted on the walls of Paleolithic caves remind us of just how old this way of seeing and thinking may be.

So here's to the dreamer, Ivan, who understands the language of birds! May he enjoy life with his wise princess in the kingdom beside the blue sea. And may we all, too, in our own journeys, come at last to that good land.

Text copyright © 2000 by Rafe Martin. Illustrations copyright © 2000 by Susan Gaber. All rights reserved. This book, or parts thereof, may not be reproduced in any form without permission in writing from the publisher. G. P. Putnam's Sons, a division of Penguin Putnam Books for Young Readers, 345 Hudson Street, New York, NY 10014. G. P. Putnam's Sons, Reg. U.S. Pat. & Tm. Off. Published simultaneously in Canada. Printed in Hong Kong by South China Printing Co. (1988) Ltd. Designed by Gunta Alexander. Text set in Phaistos. The art was done in acrylics on bristol board.
Library of Congress Cataloging-in-Publication Data Martin, Rafe, 1946– The language of birds / Rafe Martin ; illustrated by Susan Gaber. p. cm. Summary: A retelling of the Russian tale about a wealthy merchant's younger son who proves his worth in an unusual way. [1. Folklore—Russia.] I. Gaber, Susan, ill. II. Title. PZ8.1.M3725LAn 2000 [398.2'0947'02]—dc21 98-48917 CIP AC
ISBN 0-399-22925-6 10 9 8 7 6 5 4 3 2 1 First Impression